Dig and Tip

Written by Samantha Montgomerie

Collins

This pit is big.

The bucket will dig.

This bucket cuts.

It sinks in.

Lots of them dig.

They dig this pit.

This job is big.

This is quick.

Bang! Thud!

It is quick to tip.

15

Letters and Sounds: Phase 3

Word count: 40

Focus phonemes: /j/ /w/ /z/ /th/ /ng/ /nk/ /qu/

Common exception words: of, and, pulls, they, the, to

Curriculum links: Understanding the world

Early learning goals: Reading: read and understand simple sentences; use phonic knowledge to decode regular words and read them aloud accurately; read some common irregular words

Developing fluency

- Your child may enjoy hearing you read the book.
- Take turns to read a double page, encouraging your child to reread a sentence if they have difficulties. On page 12, read **Bang!** and **Thud!** together with emphasis. If necessary, point out the exclamation marks, and explain how these mean the words need extra emphasis.

Phonic practice

- Focus on the two syllable words, and ask your children to clap out the syllables as they read the words slowly:

  zig-zags   buck-et

- Turn to page 7 and challenge your child to identify the pair of letters that make one sound in **sinks**. (*nk*) Repeat for **Bang** and **Thud** on page 12. (*ng, th*)
- Look at the "I spy sounds" pages (14–15) together. Ask your child to find words that contain the sounds /z/ and /j/. Prompt them by pointing to the zigzag-shaped road on page 15 and saying: Zigzags. "Zigzags" is a /z/ word. Point to the woman jogging and say: The woman is jogging. "Jog" is a /j/ word.

Extending vocabulary

- Focus on the meaning of **pulls** on pages 4–5. Ask your child:
  - What can you **pull**? (e.g. *a rope, a weed out of the soil*)
  - Can you think of a word with the opposite meaning? (*push, pushes*)